To Amanda.

IN THE NIGHT KITCHEN

MAURICE SENDAK

IN THE NIGHT KITCHEN

MAURICE SENDAK

RED FOX

A Red Fox Book

Published by Random House Children's Books
61-63 Uxbridge Road, London W5 5SA

A division of The Random House Group Ltd
London Melbourne Sydney Auckland
Johannesburg and agencies throughout the world

Copyright © Maurice Sendak 1970

7 9 10 8

First published in Great Britain by The Bodley Head Children's Books 1971

Red Fox edition 2001

Printed in China by Midas Printing Limited

THE RANDOM HOUSE GROUP Limited Reg. No. 954009

www.kidsatrandomhouse.co.uk

ISBN 978 0 099 41747 7
(from January 2007)
0 099 41747 2

FOR SADIE AND PHILIP

DID YOU EVER HEAR OF MICKEY, HOW HE HEARD A RACKET IN THE NIGHT

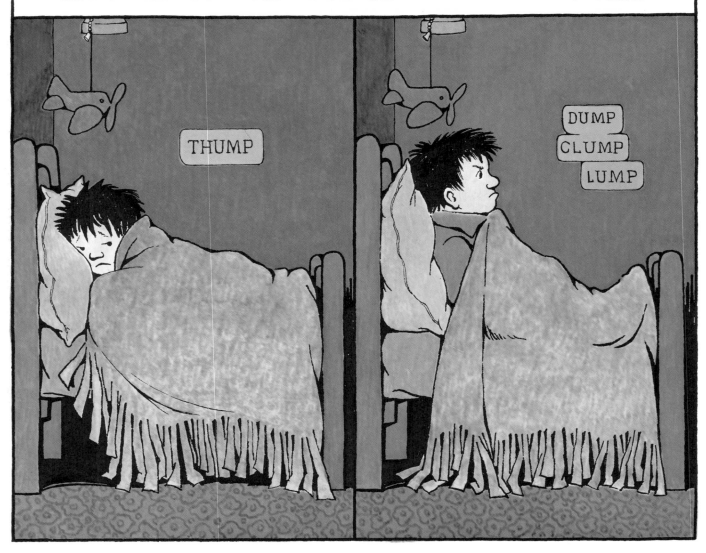

AND FELL THROUGH THE DARK, OUT OF HIS CLOTHES

AND THEY PUT THAT BATTER UP TO BAKE

A DELICIOUS MICKEY-CAKE.

SO HE SKIPPED FROM THE OVEN & INTO BREAD DOUGH
ALL READY TO RISE IN THE NIGHT KITCHEN.

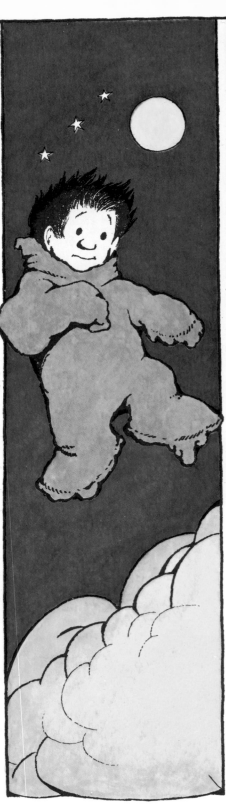

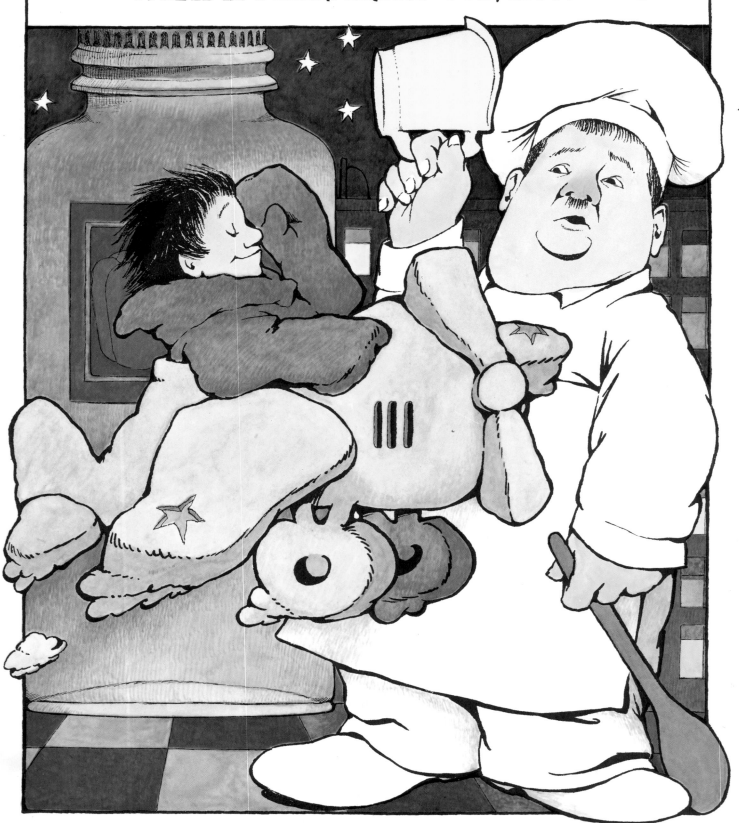

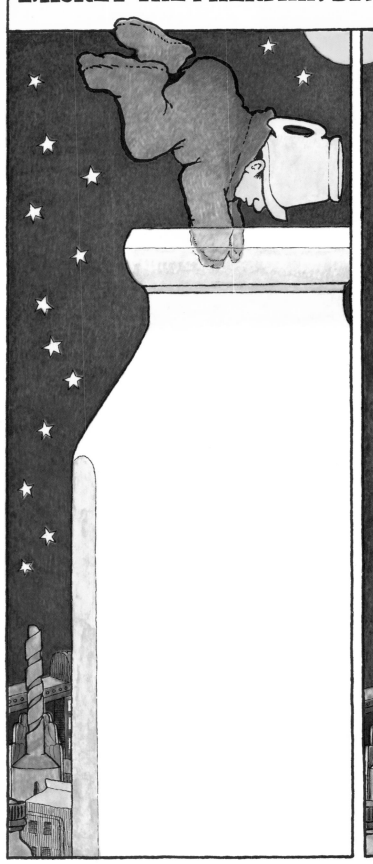

THEN HE SWAM TO THE TOP, POURING MILK FROM HIS CUP INTO BATTER BELOW—

SO THE BAKERS THEY MIXED IT
AND BEAT IT AND BAKED IT.

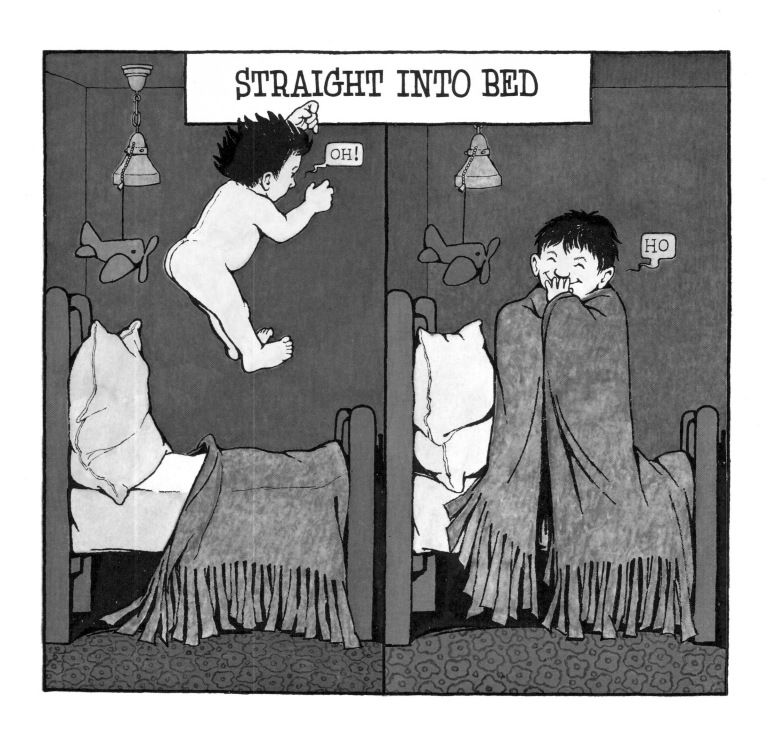

AND THAT'S WHY, THANKS TO MICKEY — WE HAVE CAKE EVERY MORNING